SWIM
OR SINK

BY JAKE MADDOX

text by
Brandon Terrell

STONE ARCH BOOKS
a capstone imprint

Jake Maddox JV books are published by
Stone Arch Books
a Capstone imprint
1710 Roe Crest Drive
North Mankato, Minnesota 56003

www.capstonepub.com

Library of Congress Cataloging-in-Publication Data
Names: Maddox, Jake, author. | Terrell, Brandon, 1978- author. | Maddox, Jake.
 Jake Maddox JV.
Title: Swim or sink / by Jake Maddox ; text by Brandon Terrell.
Description: North Mankato, Minnesota : Stone Arch Books, [2019] | Series: Jake Maddox.
 Jake Maddox JV | Summary: Although only in eighth grade, Baxter Reilly is an important
 member of the Edgeview High School in Tempe, Arizona, and lately the pool has been his
 place of refuge from the stress of his parents' separation. But now, between the pending
 divorce, his father's miserable apartment, his mother's new boyfriend, and the resentment
 and bullying from his older teammates, it is getting harder to focus on his role as the
 anchor of the 400 freestyle relay in the upcoming races.
Identifiers: LCCN 2019008760| ISBN 9781496584632 (hardcover) | ISBN 9781496584656
 (paperback) | ISBN 9781496584670 (ebook pdf)
Subjects: LCSH: Swimming—Juvenile fiction. | Swim teams—Juvenile fiction. | Teamwork
 (Sports)—Juvenile fiction. | Children of separated parents—Juvenile fiction. | Bullying—
 Juvenile fiction. | Contests—Juvenile fiction. | Distraction (Psychology)—Juvenile fiction.
 | Tempe (Ariz.)—Juvenile fiction. | CYAC: Swimming—Fiction. | Teamwork (Sports)—
 Fiction. | Divorce—Fiction. | Bullying—Fiction. | Tempe (Ariz.)—Fiction. | LCGFT:
 Sports fiction.
Classification: LCC PZ7.M25643 Sv 2019 | DDC 813.6 [Fic] —dc23
LC record available at https://lccn.loc.gov/2019008760

Designer: Dina Her

Photo Credits: Shutterstock: Andrey Armyagov, design element, Brocreative, design element,
cluckva (geometric), design element, Solis Images, Cover

TABLE OF CONTENTS

CHAPTER 1
THE CALM AND THE CURRENT............5

CHAPTER 2
A NEW HOME............15

CHAPTER 3
RELAY TEAM REVEALED............23

CHAPTER 4
FEELING ADRIFT............31

CHAPTER 5
DINNER DATE?............39

CHAPTER 6
PRELIM PRESSURE............47

CHAPTER 7
PRESSING ONWARD............55

CHAPTER 8
THE TRUTH COMES OUT............61

CHAPTER 9
POOLSIDE CHAT............67

CHAPTER 10
PART OF A TEAM............73

CHAPTER 11
A FLOOD OF MEMORIES............81

CHAPTER I

THE CALM AND THE CURRENT

Baxter Reilly's muscles tensed. His toes curled over the lip of the starting block. He stared down at the crisp blue water through his goggles and waited for the starting whistle.

This was his favorite moment of racing. The electricity coursed through his veins. He waited, ready to spring into motion.

From across the school's aquatic center, Coach Li blew a sharp blast on his whistle. The sound rang through the air. Baxter dove headfirst into the pool.

His body slipped under the cold water. He stayed under as long as he could, propelling himself forward with his arms and legs. The longer he remained underwater, the faster he moved.

Finally, when he could no longer hold his breath, Baxter broke the surface. He started the rhythmic arm movements of the front crawl.

On either side of him were other members of the Edgeview varsity swim team. They were all in high school, whereas Baxter was still in eighth grade. But at Edgeview, the best swimmers made the top team. Grade level didn't matter.

And Baxter knew how to swim.

He'd loved the water since he was five. One of his earliest memories was of seeing the ocean for the very first time. His mom and dad had driven him from their home in Tempe, Arizona, to Los Angeles, California.

Baxter remembered the feeling of the sun on his face, reflecting off the ocean waves. He remembered flipping off his shoes and racing across the beach to the water. He could see his parents dancing together in the sand. He remembered the thrill of being tossed up by the waves.

And he remembered the undercurrent pulling him down, down, down. How it held him under until his dad grabbed the back of his shirt and pulled him safely to the surface.

He remembered that most of all, because in that moment, he didn't have control. The water let him know that there was something much larger at work beneath the surface. The calm, and the current.

Baxter shook himself free of the memory. If he thought too much about his family and everything they'd been through over the past six months, it would affect his focus. He had to concentrate on his swimming now.

The end of the pool drew close. Baxter started a perfect flip turn. He dipped deeper in the water and twisted his body in a somersault.

His feet hit the side of the pool perfectly. Baxter bent his knees and shoved off the side wall, heading back the way he came.

He was focused on his own breathing and swim strokes. He didn't know how his teammates were doing. He reached out and felt his fingers touch the lip of the pool.

As he took off his goggles, he saw he was one of the first swimmers to complete the lap. Two lanes down, Clark Daniels stood watching him, goggles and swim cap already off.

"Nice work, Baxter and Clark!" Coach Li said. "That's how you do it, boys!"

The swim team's coach paced along the side of the pool in his shorts and tank top. He always wore his hair slicked back, making it look like he'd just gotten out of the water. Once upon a time, Coach Li was an alternate for the U.S. Olympic Swim Team. Now he taught health class at the high school. But he still had the competitive spirit of an Olympian.

"Good work, team!" Coach Li said when the rest of the swimmers had finished the lap. "You've all shown a great deal of improvement. Some more than others." Coach Li looked over and made eye contact with Baxter.

Coach continued. "With section finals on the horizon, we all really need to put our focus into each swim. I need to decide who will race in each event, so Monday at practice, I'll assign races for each of you. Expect a few . . . surprises."

Coach Li blew the whistle again. That signaled the end of practice.

Baxter pushed himself up out of the water and sat on the pool's edge. Next to him, his friend Tayvon did the same.

"Man," Tayvon said, "I hate surprises."

Baxter wrung out his swim cap over the pool. "Yeah, me too."

"My family had a surprise party for my grams on her eightieth birthday," Tayvon shook his head.

"Let's just say it didn't go well." He held his chest, then fell back to the pool deck with his tongue hanging out.

Baxter shot him a look. "Dude, I've met your grandma. You didn't surprise her to death."

"Well sure, she's fine *now*," Tayvon said, getting to his feet. Baxter joined him. "But we ate birthday cake in the emergency room that night."

Tayvon smiled. He was short like Baxter, but he had strong legs that powered him through the water. A freshman at Edgeview, he was the closest in age to Baxter. That was probably why they hit it off. All the other guys were juniors and seniors. They towered over Baxter and Tayvon.

Clark Daniels was one of those towering guys, and his long legs and arms were pure muscle. He stood nearby with his friends Luke and Arnold. On the wall behind them was a row of banners honoring swimmers who'd medaled at past state meets. Clark's name appeared on more than one of those banners.

While Baxter and Tayvon talked poolside, Clark, Luke, and Arnold made their way toward the locker room. As they passed, Baxter felt an elbow nudge him in his chest. Not hard, but enough to throw his balance.

Baxter stepped back. He slipped on the lip of the pool and splashed down into it. Water rushed up his nose. When his feet found the bottom of the pool, he stood up in the shallow water. His eyes burned, and he began to cough.

"Whoa!" Clark said, acting surprised. "I'm so sorry. You okay, Tadpole?"

Baxter wiped the chlorine from his eyes.

"What's going on, gentlemen?" Coach Li asked. He made his way to the edge of the pool, bent down, and offered Baxter his hand. With his help, Baxter climbed out.

"Just an accident," Clark said. "I wasn't watching where I was going and bumped into our little guppy there."

Baxter clenched his jaw. It was no use getting into a fight.

"You bumped into *Baxter*," Coach Li said. He emphasized Baxter's name to correct Clark's name calling. "Are you okay?" he asked Baxter.

"Fine, Coach," Baxter said.

"Good."

But Baxter wasn't fine. He hadn't been fine since his parents told him they were "separating." That was six months ago.

Since then, Baxter had tried his hardest to keep the mess of his life outside the walls of the aquatic center. Here, in the pool, he needed to stay calm. He couldn't let anything—including Clark—get to him.

Baxter watched Clark Daniels and the rest of the team walk to the locker room, laughing and joking with one another. Coach Li remained. "Are you sure everything's okay?" he asked Baxter.

"Yes, Coach," Baxter replied. "If it's all right with you, I'd like to swim a few more laps."

Coach Li nodded. "The pool's all yours. I'll be in my office."

Baxter took a calming breath, slid his goggles back over his eyes, and dove into the water once again.

CHAPTER 2

A NEW HOME

"You're late!" Baxter's dad shouted from the open window of his car.

He blasted his horn a couple times. The sound echoed across the hot Arizona evening. Baxter's ears burned red with embarrassment as his dad smiled and waved at him. His car was parked at the curb right outside the front doors of the school.

"Dad, knock it off," he said as he opened the door. He looked over at a few of his teammates who were old enough to drive as they walked to their own cars in the parking lot. Thankfully, Clark wasn't among them. "I stayed back to swim a bit after the rest of the team finished."

"Ah," his dad said. "Scoring brownie points with the coach, eh?"

"Yeah," Baxter said quietly. "Something like that."

It was Friday, which meant he was spending the weekend at his dad's new place. It would be Baxter's first time seeing it. He hoped it was halfway decent.

At least it couldn't be worse than the crummy motel off Highway 93 where his dad had been staying. There they'd slept in a pair of twin-size beds about five feet apart from each other. Baxter's dad snored like a garbage truck. Even with earplugs, Baxter barely got any sleep.

Baxter climbed into the passenger side of the old sedan. His hair was still wet, and he could feel the T-shirt under his hoodie clinging to his back.

"How was practice?" his dad asked, cranking the wheel. The car shuddered to life as they drove out of the parking lot.

Baxter shrugged. "The usual."

"Can't believe my boy is on the *varsity* swim team." His dad shook his head in amazement. "When's the next meet?" In the orange glow from the setting sun, Baxter could see the dark circles under his dad's eyes. He looked tired. His suit coat was rumpled, his tie loose around his neck.

"We have section prelims next Thursday. How we do there determines if we make it to the section finals, and our lane placement for the race," Baxter explained. "I'm hoping to make a relay team."

His dad's sad eyes beamed proudly. "That's great!" he said.

"Are you coming to watch on Thursday?" Baxter asked. He knew the answer, though. His dad had yet to attend a meet this season.

"I'm . . . well, I'm going to do everything I can to be there," his dad replied. "Move mountains, part seas. Know what I mean?"

"Sure," Baxter mumbled.

Before long, his dad flicked on his blinker and turned into the parking lot of a small, fenced-in apartment complex. It was three stories tall, and each apartment had a narrow metal porch. Some were decorated with flags and plants, others had bikes hanging up on them.

"Welcome to Casa de Papa," his dad said. He sounded almost proud of the run-down building.

Baxter craned his head to see out the window. His nose wrinkled up.

"Don't worry," his dad added, looking over at him. "It's like me, a little rough around the edges, but warm and well intentioned. Plus, it's close to your school!"

Baxter looked at him with a blank face.

His dad put the car in park. "Come on," he said, reaching into the back seat and grabbing Baxter's bag. "Let me show you around."

They entered the fenced-in front area. A cracked sidewalk surrounded the buildings. There were two buildings, actually, the second hidden from the parking lot by the first. Between them, right in the middle of a patch of cement, was a swimming pool. The pool was filled with stagnant water that looked like it'd been in there for years.

Baxter's dad caught him looking at it. "Knew that'd grab your attention," he said, nudging Baxter.

"Not the kind of attention you're thinking, Dad," Baxter said.

His dad's apartment was on the second level. It was as small as Baxter expected. There was a cramped living room, a kitchen with a small table, and no dining room.

"Sure, it's cozy," his dad said. He clearly noticed the pained look on Baxter's face. "But hey! There are *two* bedrooms. Pretty cool, right?"

"Cool," Baxter said, unimpressed.

His dad walked over to the glass sliding door that led to the deck. He drew back the blinds like he was a real estate agent trying to make a sale. "Plus, we've got a great view of the pool."

The enthusiasm he had for his so-so apartment wasn't contagious. Baxter couldn't be excited about the place. Not when he remembered how it used to be. How they'd all been together in the house where his mom still lived.

Baxter left his gym bag in the small second bedroom. He and his dad ordered pizza and ate quietly in the kitchen. At one point, his dad held up a drooping slice of pizza and said, "Cheers to a wild Friday night, eh?"

Baxter held up his own. "Yep," he said. "Wild."

After dinner, Baxter's dad wound up on the couch in the living room—head back, mouth open, and snoring.

Meanwhile, Baxter watched the Suns basketball game and messed around on his phone. He played a few games and texted with Tayvon. The two of them talked about hanging out over the weekend. Baxter welcomed the chance to get away from his dad's new apartment.

Just thinking about the place made Baxter feel closed in. He needed to get out. Quietly, he snuck past his dad, closing the front door softly behind him. He went down the hall's faded red and patterned carpet, down the steps, and outside. He just needed some fresh air.

It was dark out now, but still warm. The city lights fought back the blanket of stars in the sky.

Baxter strolled over to the swimming pool. Surprisingly, it was lit up by a pair of underwater lights. He stripped off his socks and dipped a foot in the water.

"No way I'm going in," he muttered.

Instead, Baxter found a plastic poolside chair and sat. After sitting in the baking sun all day, the cement and the furniture gave off a nice heat. Baxter sat back, stared up at the hazy night sky, and wondered how long separations usually lasted.

CHAPTER 3

RELAY TEAM REVEALED

Baxter's weekend with his dad didn't go exactly as planned. First, Tayvon had to cancel their plans on Saturday. Then, as Baxter was drifting off to sleep that night, his earbuds playing soft music, he heard a loud slam from the next room. He removed an earbud and listened intently.

"No, that's not what I'm saying, Diane." The walls of the apartment were thin. Baxter could hear his dad's voice clearly. He was talking to Baxter's mom.

As usual, their discussion was anything but friendly. "Once again, you're twisting my words. If you'd just let me—"

Baxter popped his earbud back in and cranked up his music.

His dad must have realized that Baxter had overheard the phone call, because the following morning, there was a stack of waffles and a plate of bacon on the table. The most his dad usually made for breakfast was cereal and burnt toast.

"What do you say we go see a movie?" his dad asked. He had a wide grin on his face, but Baxter could see it wasn't quite real. "Your choice."

They spent their afternoon watching the newest *Invasion from Planet X* movie at the nicest theater in Tempe. The theater had reclining seats, and the sound was so loud it rattled Baxter's bones. It would have been the perfect escape from the cramped apartment, if his dad hadn't leaned over every few minutes, whispering, "Okay, now what's going on?"

Baxter was still feeling pretty down about the whole weekend when his dad dropped him off at Edgeview Middle School on Monday morning. "Fill that squishy brain with knowledge!" his dad said, mussing Baxter's brown hair.

Baxter went through his classes trying not to think about swim practice. Today Coach Li would assign races for the section preliminary meet. He'd said there would be some surprises. Baxter hoped that meant his hard work had earned him a spot on the relay team.

When the final bell rang that afternoon, Baxter quickly gathered his things and dashed out of school. Edgeview Middle was on the same block as the high school, so he didn't have to go far to get to the aquatic center. It was far enough, though, that he was always the last one ready for practice.

Today was no exception. Most of the team was already in the pool by the time he walked out of the locker room.

"Glad you could join us," Coach Li said. He always said it. Of course, he knew Baxter's situation and was smiling when he spoke. Still, it was just another little thing that made Baxter feel like he was out of place among his team.

Baxter stepped off the side of the pool into the water. Below the surface, he could hear the echo of the other swimmers. But it was a moment of peace, a chance to gather himself before the tough practice.

He came up, wiped the water from his face, and positioned his swim cap over his hair.

"All right, guys!" Coach Li said, clapping loudly. "Let's do this!"

They started practice by doing sets up and back across the pool. Distance swimmers practiced on one side, while Baxter joined the sprinters on the other.

Coach Li paced the length of the pool, watching them all closely and occasionally shouting out words of encouragement. More than once, he bellowed out, "Great work comes from *hard* work!" It was his favorite quote. He had it on a plaque hung above the door to the locker room.

For Baxter, the best part of practice—and swimming in general—was that he could block out whatever else was going on in his life. He could focus on the pool. On his lane. On his body movements, and the way his muscles burned.

When he'd finished the last set of laps, Baxter draped his arms over the side of the pool and rested on the lip like a fish half out of water. Other swimmers did the same.

"Okay, guys," Coach Li said. He had his clipboard now. This was the moment they'd been waiting for.

The swimmers, still floating or standing in the pool, huddled around. Coach Li stood at the edge of the pool deck and rattled off the preliminary races and the swimmers competing in them. As Baxter waited to hear if he'd made a relay team, his stomach began to feel like a lead weight pulling him down in the water.

"Tayvon and Baxter," Coach Li called out. "One hundred freestyle."

"Cool," Tayvon said. He swam up next to Baxter and offered a fist bump. One hundred meant two laps down and back in the pool. Freestyle meant they could use whatever stroke they wanted to. His placement in the race wasn't a surprise. And neither were any of the other individual races.

But then, as he prepared to list off the names for the final event, the 400 freestyle relay, Coach Li paused. "Okay," he said. "Here's where we made a couple of changes based on what I've been seeing this season. I needed my fastest swimmers in the first and last spots of the relay. So with that in mind, the four swimmers in the free relay are: Clark, Luke, Arnold, and in the anchor position . . . Baxter."

"Yes!" Baxter slapped the water with his hands, spraying himself and the swimmers around him.

"A little excited, are we?" Coach Li asked. When Baxter looked up, he saw the smiling coach wiping water off his face. A large wet spot covered the front of his shirt.

"Oops," Baxter said. "Sorry."

"The meet is a week from Thursday," Coach Li continued. "How we do there determines where we stand at section finals that weekend. The top eight teams will compete at sections for a shot at going to the state tournament next month. So I don't really have to tell you how important it is to stay focused right now. No distractions."

As Coach Li finished his speech, Baxter could feel every set of eyes in the aquatic center focus on him. Especially Clark Daniels'. Baxter glanced over at Clark, who was sitting on the edge of the pool three lanes away. Sure enough, his eyes were locked squarely on Baxter.

"All right!" Coach Li tossed the clipboard down, and it clattered on the tile floor. "Everyone back in the pool. Let's practice for prelims."

CHAPTER 4

FEELING ADRIFT

Baxter spent the next hour with Tayvon, taking turns and practicing their freestyle laps in one of the lanes. Both used the front crawl. It was the most common stroke in the freestyle and the fastest.

As he moved quickly down and back in the pool, Baxter did his best to forget the way Clark had looked at him after his name had been called as relay anchor. Fear was creeping up inside him, and he tried hard to push it back down.

He deserved a place on the relay team. Obviously, Coach Li felt the same way.

"Okay, relay teams!" Coach Li called out as Baxter finished his last lap. "Practice in lanes three and four!"

Baxter climbed out of the water, and the fear he'd been pushing down suddenly washed over him again. His hands began to shake, and his teeth chattered despite the aquatic center's hot, humid air.

The other three relay swimmers were already lined up near lane three. Luke, Arnold, and Clark loomed like skyscrapers as Baxter joined them.

Clark glared down at him. "You better not slow us down, Tadpole," he said.

Coach Li blew his whistle, and Clark dove into the water. He was a fast, dynamic swimmer. He quickly completed his laps, touching the wall just as Luke dove in.

Luke powered through his front crawl, followed by Arnold.

Baxter stepped up on the block, preparing for his turn. His legs felt rubbery, and his whole body shook. He felt more nervous now than during meets, when he had bleachers full of people cheering him on.

Arnold glided in on his last lap. As he touched the wall, Baxter pushed himself off the starting block.

He hit the water, staying under as long as possible. This time, though, he pushed himself harder than usual.

He broke the surface and started his crawl. Down, in, up. Down, in, up. His arms worked in a steady rhythm. Each time he twisted his head to breathe, he could hear Tayvon and a few others cheering him on.

But then, snatches of his parents' angry phone call from Saturday night suddenly rattled his brain.

"That's not what I'm saying, Diane. . . ."

He saw the plate of apology waffles.

He felt the thin walls of his dad's shoebox apartment creeping in on him.

Baxter tried to regain his focus, but with each stroke, the water felt thicker. Each breath became a short gasp for air.

On the last stretch, yards away from the wall, Baxter reached out his hand. When he touched, he heard Coach Li blast his whistle again.

Baxter pulled off his goggles and looked at the other relay swimmers. They were all staring at Coach Li, waiting to hear their time.

"How'd we do?" Clark asked.

"There's definitely room for improvement," Coach Li said. Baxter winced.

Clark clapped his hands in frustration. "Well, I know it wasn't the three of us," he said, pointing at himself, Luke, and Arnold.

"Listen," Coach Li said. "You're a team. You win as a team, you lose as one. Try it again. You've got until next Thursday to shave off some time."

Baxter climbed out of the water. He and Coach Li locked eyes, and Coach gave him a slight nod.

Coach Li had faith Baxter could succeed. But if the last practice race was any sign, Baxter was starting to wonder if his mind was too far adrift to anchor the team.

*   *   *

After practice, Baxter showered in the locker room and dressed by himself. The other guys on the team had assigned lockers from gym class. But since Baxter went to Edgeview Middle, they'd given him a spare locker way in the back.

Some days it bothered him to be stuck in the back corner, away from the rest of the team. But after the practice he'd just had, Baxter was grateful for the privacy of his out-of-the-way locker.

Baxter checked his phone to see if his mom was waiting outside for him. As he shrugged on his thin coat and shouldered his gym bag, he heard footsteps rounding the corner.

Baxter looked up to see Clark standing there. The senior leaned up against the nearest bank of lockers, hands in his pockets.

"Um . . . hey," Baxter said. He wanted to walk away, but Clark blocked the only path out.

"So you know all those banners on the walls by the pool?" Clark asked. There was an edge to his voice.

"Yeah," Baxter said quietly.

"You know whose name is on a lot of those banners?" Clark said.

"Um . . . yours?"

"Correct." Clark leaned forward. He slid his hand out of his pocket and pointed at his own chest. "*My* name. And as a senior, this is my *last* chance to go to state for relay. My last chance to hang another banner on that wall. And right now, the only thing that seems to be getting in my way of that is *you*. Understand?"

Baxter nodded. He couldn't maintain eye contact with Clark.

"Tadpole, you're a small fish in a big pool," Clark said. "Better learn to swim."

He turned on a heel and disappeared into the shadows of the locker room, leaving Baxter alone.

CHAPTER 5

DINNER DATE?

"Honey? Honey, are you listening to me?"

Baxter's mom walked past his bedroom door again. Her baby blue dress fluttered behind her. He lay on his bed, head on the pillow. His algebra textbook rested on his chest. He was hoping that the information would just sink into him.

"What, Mom?" Baxter hollered.

His mom appeared back in his doorframe. She sighed and said, "I asked if you were listening to me. I clearly have my answer."

It was the following evening, and Baxter had just gotten home from another frustrating swim practice.

The wall he'd built to separate swimming from his outside life had been cracked by the memory of his parents' argument. But the pressure applied by Clark had nearly crumbled it. Baxter couldn't seem to find a rhythm anymore, and his laps were sloppy.

Right now, though, Baxter wanted to hole himself up in his bedroom. He was safe there. It was the room he'd had since he was a baby. The walls were plastered with posters of famous swimmers, musicians, and artists. A shelf next to the desk held trophies and medals from all of his junior varsity and city swim team meets.

"Sorry," Baxter said. "I was too busy focusing on my homework."

"The homework that's currently sleeping on your chest?" his mom asked.

Baxter scooped up the book and pretended to read it. "I was taking a moment to . . . uh, think through this equation." He looked over the top of the book. His mom stood with her arms crossed. She clearly wasn't buying it.

"Baxter, I'll only be gone a couple of hours at this work dinner," his mom explained. "But you'll have to fend for yourself. There are leftovers in the fridge, okay?"

Baxter gave her a mock salute. "Roger that," he replied.

"Now where did I put those earrings?" she muttered, tugging at one ear lobe. With that, she was off again.

Just hearing about dinner was enough to make Baxter's stomach growl. He flipped the book off his belly and stood up. "Lead the way," he said to his stomach, patting it.

Baxter's bedroom was on the second floor, so he started down the stairs. On the wall to his left, there was a series of framed family photographs. Baxter remembered the day his parents had hung them.

They'd measured each one out, picking which photo would go where. His dad had hit his thumb with the hammer because he's a terrible handyman.

Looking at the photos as he walked down the steps, Baxter saw his family the way they used to be. Christmas morning. Birthdays. Even a photo of them in front of the ocean from the trip to California. They were smiling in every photo, a perfect trio of happiness.

Now, though . . .

When he reached the kitchen, Baxter opened the refrigerator door and poked around inside. His mom was a health nut. The crispers were filled with fresh fruit and vegetables, and there were glass containers of leftover pasta and salads.

"Definitely no pizza or popcorn here," Baxter mumbled. Finally, he pulled out a container of rice and grilled chicken.

"Baxter?" his mom called from upstairs. "Is my phone down there? I can't find it anywhere."

Baxter popped the container into the microwave. "Nah, I don't think so," he said. He gave the dining room and kitchen area a once-over.

But then he heard a buzz coming from under a stack of newspapers. The buzz came again, and Baxter spied the corner of his mom's phone sticking out. He took it from beneath the papers. He was about to call out to her that he'd found it—

—and stopped.

When Baxter had lifted the buzzing phone up, the screen had come to life. It showed a text message from a contact listed as *Mark Cell.*

It read: *Just pulled up in driveway. Will wait here for you.*

"Who's Mark?" Baxter asked himself.

His mind began to race. His mom had never mentioned a coworker named Mark before. Was she lying to him? What if she wasn't going out for a work dinner? What if she was actually going on a *date*? Was that allowed during a separation?

Baxter wanted to tap the text. He wanted to see what else this Mark guy and his mom had been chatting about. But then he heard footsteps coming down the stairs and quickly stashed the phone back under the newspaper.

"Seriously," his mom said as she entered the kitchen. "I can't find the thing *anywhere*."

"Well, you've got a ton of papers there," Baxter said. He casually pointed at the crossword puzzle. "Maybe it's buried under that stack?"

His mom lifted up the paper. "Aha!" she exclaimed. "Here it is. Good call, Bax."

Baxter saw her check the phone and see the message. She quickly dropped the phone into her purse. "Okay, gotta run." She came over to Baxter and gave him a peck on the forehead. "Be good, finish your homework, and don't run out chasing supervillains. Got it?"

"Got it," Baxter answered quietly. He couldn't muster up a smile.

His mom reached the front door, turned around, and blew him a kiss. "Bye, sweetie!"

He waved but didn't pretend to catch the kiss like he used to as a kid. Instead, he just stood there. Stood there as she closed the door behind her. Stood there as the microwave beeped to tell him his dinner was hot. Stood there as the sound of a car driving away drifted in through an open window.

CHAPTER 6

PRELIM PRESSURE

Swim meets were always loud affairs. Teams, parents, family, and friends all yelled as loudly as they could, cheering for their school. But on preliminary night, there was an extra charge in the air.

Baxter felt it as he walked into the aquatic center at Fountain Hills High, a school in a suburb near Tempe. Only the top eight swimmers in each event would advance to the section finals on Saturday. The rest would be done for the season.

As if that wasn't enough to worry about, Baxter hadn't been able to stop thinking about the text message his mother had received from that Mark guy.

He had always thought his parents' separation would eventually end and they would get back together. But that was before he'd heard the way they yelled at each other on the phone. And before his mom's "work" dinner.

Baxter didn't say a word on the rowdy bus ride over. He was silent while the team dressed in the locker room, while they shrugged on matching giant parkas over their swimsuits to stay warm. He said nothing as they walked out into the loud pool deck, where Coach Li gave them a pep talk before the teams were introduced.

Baxter scanned the crowd for his parents and saw his mom, sitting in the bleachers alone.

His dad was not there. Again.

"Hey, man," Tayvon said. He came up next to Baxter and bumped his shoulder. "Relax. You got this."

"Yeah, sure," Baxter said.

As the meet began, the teams took their places along the pool. With each race, they stood around the edge, hooting and hollering and slapping the tiled floor.

Clark swam his way into section finals in both the 50 freestyle and the 100 backstroke. Luke touched the wall just ahead of his competitors in the 200 butterfly.

"Next event is the 100 freestyle," a voice over the PA system said.

"That's us, dude," Tayvon said. He let out a deep breath and started flapping his arms wildly to get warmed up.

Baxter did the same, slapping his palms on his thighs. Then they slipped the parkas off and approached the blocks.

Baxter was in lane five, Tayvon in lane two. The eight swimmers in their heat all stepped up onto their blocks together. "Swimmers on your mark," the announcer said.

Baxter looked over at his mom, just a quick glance. She wasn't looking back. Instead, she was talking with a man seated in the row behind her. As Baxter watched, she laughed at something the man said. It made him think of the text again, the one from Mark. Whoever *that* was.

A buzzer split the air of the aquatic center, catching Baxter off guard. His focus had slipped at the worst possible moment!

Baxter quickly dove into the pool, a split second behind the others. He propelled himself underwater with his legs, keeping his body straight. Then he broke the surface and started his stroke.

As he turned his head to breathe, he saw the swimmer in the lane next to him. He was way ahead of Baxter. If Baxter wanted to catch up, he was going to have to push himself.

He reached the end of the pool and somersaulted to head back in the other direction. Stroke after stroke, Baxter swam as hard as he could. But judging by the swimmers around him, he was too far behind to catch up.

When the race was over, Baxter touched the side of the pool and stood up. He finished in last place. He hadn't qualified for the 100 freestyle.

Baxter tore his swim cap and goggles off and chucked them onto the pool deck. From his spot in lane two, Tayvon looked over at Baxter with sympathy.

"Don't worry," Tayvon said after they'd climbed out of the pool. Tayvon had finished in third place in the heat and would almost certainly qualify for the section finals. "You've still got the relay. You can bounce back."

"Sure," Baxter said quietly. He looked over at his mom. She was looking back at him with concern.

The 400 freestyle relay was the last event of the meet. There were two heats. Sixteen teams looking to fill eight lanes at the section meet. The Edgeview team watched the first heat while they went through their warm-up routines.

When the announcer called for swimmers in the second heat to take their places, Clark motioned for Baxter with his head.

"Get in here, Tadpole," Clark said. He pulled the four of them close. "Look, all we have to do is place eighth overall and we're in. But the better the time, the better the lane placement at section finals. So I want to *win* this thing."

"You know it," Luke said.

"Like Coach says," Arnold added, "great work comes from hard work."

Baxter remained silent.

The team lined up, and Clark stood on the block. When the buzzer sounded, he dove into the water.

"Edgeview! Edgeview! Edgeview!" the team chanted. Baxter didn't join in. He was intently watching Clark.

Clark pulled into a strong lead—one that Luke and Arnold maintained. When Arnold made his last turn and started back, Baxter took his position on the block. He crouched, placing his hands on the lip of the block.

As Arnold reached out to touch the edge, images fluttered into Baxter's head. His mom whisking out the front door, happy as can be. His dad asleep and alone on an apartment couch. The family photo of the three of them at the beach.

Baxter wobbled on the block. His hand slipped forward, and he fell face-first into the pool!

CHAPTER 7

PRESSING ONWARD

Baxter threw his arms out just in time to clumsily dive into the water. He sucked in a breath as he went under. Water rushed up his nose. He came to the surface, flailing and listening for the whistle that would disqualify the team.

It didn't come. *Arnold must have touched the side before I fell in*, Baxter thought. That meant they were still in the race.

Baxter straightened out his body and sliced through the water.

He needed to get this race back on track. If they didn't make it to the section finals, his team—Clark especially—would never let him forget it. But he needed to focus.

The teams on either side of him had caught up. He'd lost the lead Clark and the others had worked hard to achieve.

It was up to Baxter to gain it back.

He swam as fast as he could. He pushed himself until his lungs felt like they were being squeezed shut. Each stroke made his muscles ache, but he pressed onward.

The flashes—his mom, his dad, his life before it was turned upside down—came hurtling back. But he tried hard to brush them off. *Concentrate*, he told himself. *Every yard matters.*

Baxter made the last flip turn, shoving his feet hard off the pool's side. When he came up, he saw he'd caught up to the other racers. Twenty yards. Fifteen. Ten.

Baxter kicked hard, swinging his arm up—five—
and reaching out for the—two—side of the pool—
one—and—

Got it!

He'd made it! Baxter stood up in the pool and
looked around. . . .

Half of the other racers in their heat had already
finished. His heart sunk. It looked like their chances
of making the section finals were done.

Baxter glanced up at his team, but they were all
staring at the large electronic board where times were
displayed.

The numbers next to Edgeview flickered, and a
time appeared: 3:17:24. Eighth place overall.

They'd made it. *Barely.* They were the last team to
qualify for the section finals. But they were in.

Baxter climbed out of the water. He felt he should
be happy, but he knew his teammates were upset
with him. If it weren't for him, they'd be on top of the
board.

Clark stepped up to Baxter and looked down on him. "What the heck were you doing out there, Tadpole?" he asked under his breath.

"Yeah," Luke added. "We should have had the best lane placement at section finals, but because of you, we'll have the worst."

Baxter didn't want to talk to anyone. "But at least we'll be there," he said, walking away.

"No thanks to *you*," Clark said.

Baxter couldn't stop himself. He turned toward Clark, his hands balled into fists. He didn't care if the rest of the aquatic center was watching.

Coach Li stepped between them. He held out a parka to Baxter, who stopped cold in his tracks. "Rocky race there, Baxter," he said. "I imagine you'll work out the kinks by Saturday?"

Baxter took the parka, gripped it hard with both hands. "Yeah, Coach," he said, putting it on and walking away from Clark. He leaned against the wall near Tayvon.

"Hey," Tayvon said. "We'll both be swimming at section finals. Congrats."

Baxter chewed his lip and tried to hold back tears. "Thanks, man," he said.

CHAPTER 8

THE TRUTH COMES OUT

"Wow! That was *amazing!*" Baxter's mom flailed her arms wildly as they walked out to the car. The rest of the team was heading back from Fountain Hills on the bus, but Baxter decided he'd rather ride home with his mom. "You had it, then you didn't, then you fought your way back . . ." She moved her arms in a terrible impression of a front crawl. ". . . and *bam!* Section finals, here we come."

"Yeah," Baxter said quietly. "Yay, us."

His mom studied him for a moment. Finally, she dug through her purse for her set of car keys. "I know why you're bummed," she said. "If your dad could have been here, you know he'd have been the loudest person in there. He just . . . had to work."

Baxter shook his head. His mom had totally misread his mood. For once, he hadn't been thinking of his dad. After she mentioned him, though, his words from their weekend together came rushing back.

Move mountains, his dad had told him. *Part seas.* Another lie.

"Work?" Baxter said. "That's one of the oldest, lamest excuses in the book, Mom."

"Well, it's the truth." It wasn't. Baxter could tell.

"Maybe he had a *work dinner*," Baxter said. The words tumbled out before he could stop them.

"What do you mean by that?" His mom looked surprised, like she'd been caught red-handed. And that was when Baxter realized his fears had been right. She'd been lying to him. The dinner with Mark *had* been a date.

"Nothing," Baxter grumbled.

They rode home in silence. When they reached the house, Baxter took his gym bag right up to his room and dropped it on the floor. He closed the door behind him. All he wanted to do was shower and fall into his pillow.

Unfortunately, his mom had other plans. She rapped lightly on his door. "Bax, hon?" she said softly. "Open up."

He sighed. "Can it wait?" he asked.

"I don't think so."

He opened the door, and she walked in. She sat on the edge of his bed and wrung her hands nervously.

Baxter read her body language. *This is it. This is the conversation.*

"Baxter, have a seat, dear." His mom patted the bed next to her, and he sat. "I know the past few months have been hard on you," she said.

"Understatement," he muttered.

"That's fair. It's been tough for you. I get that. And judging by what you said in the car . . . you're right," she said. "I haven't been honest with you."

"You didn't have a work dinner, did you?" Baxter asked.

His mom shook her head. "Baxter dear, your father and I . . . well, we've decided to complete the separation process."

Baxter crinkled up his nose. "What did you call it?" he asked.

"We're completing the separation process," his mom repeated.

"Divorce," Baxter said, louder than he expected. "What you mean is you're getting a divorce."

"Baxter . . ."

"It's a divorce. *Di-vorce*. Say the word, Mom. You're already ruining my life. You don't have to be a coward about it too," Baxter said.

He didn't want to hear any more. Baxter wasn't

sure where he was going to go, but he needed to get out of the house. *Anywhere* was better than being in this room, having this conversation.

Baxter stood up. He saw his gym bag still lying on the floor where he'd dropped it and scooped it up with one hand.

"Sit back down," his mom ordered him.

"No."

"Where do you think you're going, then, Baxter?" she asked.

Baxter shrugged. "I'll figure it out," he said. "I guess I'm just completing the separation process."

With that, he stormed out of his room, stomping down the stairs. His mom called his name behind him. Baxter didn't look back. He reached the bottom of the stairs, left, and slammed the door behind him.

CHAPTER 9

POOLSIDE CHAT

Baxter sank to the bottom of the pool. It was quiet, peaceful. He had his eyes closed, trying his hardest to shut out the rest of the world. Trying to stay calm and not let the current carry him away.

But the conversation with his mom flooded his mind. *Complete the separation process. Divorce. You're already ruining my life. You don't have to be a coward about it.*

Baxter opened his mouth and screamed as loud as he could underwater. His anger turned to bubbles.

When he couldn't hold his breath any longer, Baxter floated to the surface. As he came up from underwater, his eyes closed, he heard a voice.

"Yeah, he's here. I've got him."

Baxter wiped the water from his eyes and turned his head. His dad was sitting in one of the chairs beside the pool. He had his cell phone to his ear.

"Sure thing," he said into the phone. "I'll bring him by in the morning before school."

He hung up, placing the phone on the chair next to him. "Nice night for a swim," he said to Baxter.

When Baxter had stormed out of his mom's house, he had no plan for where he was going. But after a fifteen-minute bus ride, he had found himself outside his dad's apartment building. Too embarrassed to go up to the door, he'd instead stripped off his shirt and jumped into the pool in his gym shorts.

Now that he'd been busted, Baxter swam to the side of the pool, then climbed up the small ladder barely bolted into the side of the crummy pool.

His dad had been kind enough to bring a towel down with him. It was one of Baxter's childhood towels, thin and ragged, with a cartoon of Ninja Mummy on it. Baxter's dad tossed it over to him, and he caught it, wrapping it around his shoulders.

Baxter sat in the chair beside his dad. For a brief moment, he remembered the time he and his parents visited his aunt Karen in Iowa when he was ten. They'd stayed at a hotel, and his dad had thrown him high in the air while in the hotel pool. Baxter splashed down hard every time. His mom sat in a chair with her book and laughed from under an umbrella.

"Your mom told you, eh?" his dad asked.

Baxter nodded. "She said you were 'completing the separation process.'"

His dad made a face. "Those were her exact words?"

"Exact."

His dad shook his head. "Yikes. Makes us sound like we're a pair of NASA robots or something."

This made Baxter smile.

"Listen," his dad continued. "I want you to know this isn't your fault, Baxter."

"I know."

"You may feel like—wait, what?"

"I'm not dumb, Dad. I know it's not my fault," said Baxter. "I saw the looks you gave each other. I heard the fights after I'd gone to bed."

"Oh." His dad turned away at the sound of a car in the parking lot.

"I assumed you'd figure it out, though," Baxter said. "Get back together and stop taking it out on me."

"Taking it out on you?" His dad sounded confused.

"Dad," Baxter explained, "I had the biggest swim meet of my life tonight. You weren't there to see it."

"Oh," his dad said. "Well, your mom and I have decided that being in the same space together isn't something we can handle right now. We'll get there someday, I'm sure. Just not yet."

"Do you know how selfish that is?" Baxter could

feel himself getting angry again. He stood, pulled the towel from around his shoulders, and threw it down on the chair.

"Hey," his dad said, also standing. "This is hard for all of us, Baxter."

"Well, I can't stop thinking about it. It's affecting my life. I nearly ruined my chance to swim at the section finals." Tears stung the sides of his eyes, and Baxter wiped them away with his fists.

Baxter's dad put his hands on his hips and sighed. "I'll talk with her. I'll tell her how you're feeling about everything. I promise."

Baxter nodded. "I don't care if you hate each other," he said. "Just stop acting like you hate me too."

And then the tears came in one heaving sob. It was so unexpected that Baxter couldn't hold them back. He covered his face with both hands. Baxter's dad stepped over and wrapped his arms around him, holding him tight.

They stood that way for a very long time.

CHAPTER 10

PART OF A TEAM

Saturday morning, the day of the section finals, Baxter's mom made him a large breakfast. "You can't swim on an empty stomach," she told him. She smiled and slid a bowl of yogurt in front of him, along with a plate of banana slices, orange wedges, and cut strawberries.

Baxter knew what was up. They hadn't talked about what happened the night of the prelims, and his mom was doing whatever she could to act like it hadn't happened. And that was fine . . . for now. Baxter had other things to worry about.

The section finals meet was held at Tempe University. The aquatic center was a large building in the middle of campus with tall windows on all sides.

Baxter's mom walked in with him. "Good luck, hon," his mom said to him. "I'll be cheering as loud as I can."

"Thanks, Mom," Baxter said quietly.

Baxter's mom reached out and put a hand on his shoulder. "I talked to your dad last night," she said. She'd always been good at reading Baxter's mind. "He'll make it if he can."

They went their separate ways—Baxter to find the locker room and his mom to find the pool bleachers. Baxter followed signs that directed him to where the Edgeview team was getting ready. He had one other thing to do before he could race with a clear head.

Most of the team had already arrived when Baxter found them in the locker room. Coach Li was with them, sitting on a bench. He looked up, saw Baxter, and said, "Glad you could join us."

Baxter smiled. Clark was seated at the far end of the lockers. He had one leg up on the wooden bench. It was covered in white shaving cream. Almost all the guys on the team had to shave. Smooth legs and chests make swimmers glide faster through the water.

Baxter didn't have to worry about that yet.

"Hey, man," Baxter said when he was standing in front of Clark.

Clark looked up at him. "Something I can help you with, Tadpole?"

Baxter took a deep breath. "I know how important this race is," he said. "And I know we don't get along. We don't have to like each other, but we have to work like a team. And I'm willing to do that if you are. Cool?"

Clark glared at him. Shaving cream dripped off his leg. A brief smirk curled up the side of Clark's lip, just for a second. It was so quick that Baxter wasn't even totally sure he'd seen it.

Clark made a fist and held it out to Baxter. "Cool."

Baxter bumped his fist, then turned and walked away.

The noise Baxter heard stepping out of the locker room and onto the pool deck was almost deafening. Shafts of sunlight streamed in from the towering windows. Bleachers took up one wall. On the wall opposite, a large black electronic scoreboard showed team names and race times.

Baxter studied the bleachers and found his mom sitting near the middle. She waved when they made eye contact. Then she shook her head, answering his unasked question: "Is Dad here?"

As the races began, Baxter stood cheering with the rest of his team. Section finals was the most important meet of the season. There was only one heat for each event. The top two racers or teams in each event would move on to the state meet, competing against the best swimmers in Arizona.

When the 100 freestyle racers took the blocks, a hint of envy sparked inside Baxter.

I should be competing in this race, he thought, remembering his distracted performance at prelims.

But that was behind him now. Instead of letting it bother him, Baxter joined his team and started cheering for Tayvon. He watched as his friend powered ahead of the other racers, and front crawled his way to second place.

"Congrats, dude!" Baxter high-fived Tayvon when he rejoined the team.

"That was crazy," Tayvon said. "I could even hear my grams yelling my name the whole time I was swimming!" He waved across the pool, and Baxter looked over to see an elderly woman in the front row waving back.

The other Edgeview swimmers also performed strongly. Clark swam fast and efficiently. He secured first-place finishes in both of his races.

Baxter waited patiently for the relay race, staying huddled in his parka while watching the rest of the individual races.

Then the crowd quieted and the diving teams took their turn on the other side of the aquatic center. Baxter kept checking the crowd, looking for his dad. No luck.

Finally, Coach Li gathered Baxter, Clark, Arnold, and Luke together. He said, "Okay boys, freestyle relay is up next. We've got our lane placement. We're in lane one."

Clark scoffed. "Great," he said.

"Well, what did you expect?" Luke's eyes darted over to Baxter, then back to Clark. "Eighth place gets the worst placement."

"Doesn't matter," Coach Li said. "You're in the race, right?"

No one answered.

"Right?" Coach Li repeated, louder this time.

"Right, Coach," Baxter said. The others followed his lead.

"Good. Then you've got a chance of winning. Right?" Coach said.

This time there was no hesitation. "Right," all four swimmers replied.

"Remember, great work comes from hard work." Coach Li smiled. "Now what do you say we show them how great you really are?"

CHAPTER 11

A FLOOD OF MEMORIES

The swimming pool was divided into eight lanes. Eight teams trying to win.

The three best times from the preliminary meet swam in lanes three, four, and five. They set the pace. The further out from there, the harder it was to determine how fast the other racers were going.

The teams in lanes one and eight were the worst off. They only had one swimmer to gauge their pace. The other side was a wall staring back at them.

And so, as the Edgeview freestyle relay team took their spot in lane one, Baxter knew that they had a huge obstacle to overcome. And that was on top of his other problem. If he couldn't rein in the memories that weighed him down while he swam, they'd lose for sure.

Baxter stood alongside Luke and Arnold as Clark stepped onto the block. He looked over to the crowd one last time. And there, standing at the end of the bleachers, hands in the pockets of his jeans and leaning against the wall, was his dad.

He made it, Baxter thought. *They're* both *here now.*

The buzzer sounded, and Clark dove into the water. During the prelims, Clark had given the team a strong lead. This time, though, the racers were the best of the best. Clark moved quickly down the pool and back, keeping pace with the others but never breaking free. It was a virtual tie when Luke leaped in for the second leg of the race.

"Come on, Luke!" Baxter shouted.

Clark, dripping wet, got out of the pool. He peeled off his swim cap and tossed it behind him. Arnold took his place on the starting block as Clark joined Baxter in rooting on his teammate.

Luke slipped behind a bit. The two teams in the middle lanes began to pull ahead. "Arnold, you have to make back the time," Clark said.

Arnold nodded and got into starting position. "On it."

Luke touched the wall, and Arnold started his laps. By then, the Edgeview crew was smack-dab in the middle of the pack. Arnold did all he could. He powered himself forward with each stroke. Each of his turns was perfect. The momentum was starting to shift. He was gaining on the middle lane, still three lengths behind but closing the gap.

Baxter positioned his goggles on his eyes and took his place on the block. This was it. It was time to clear his head. It was time to concentrate on the race.

We've decided to complete the separation process. . . .

Baxter heard his mom's voice in his head. He tried to push the memory away and clear his mind again. Arnold was just about to reach the pool's edge.

Baxter crouched low, saw Arnold touch, and dove into the water.

He swam underwater, straight as an arrow, before coming up. When he did, he settled right into the front crawl. Sweeping up, then down, back and over again. With each stroke, he sucked in a short burst of breath.

Whenever he came up for air, Baxter was facing the side of the pool. The other swimmers were at his back. He had no idea how he was doing.

No one watching as he flipped off his sandals and dashed into the ocean. The calm above, the current below.

The memory flickered into his mind. The time he was pulled underwater. Why was he thinking about that here? Why now? He needed to focus.

His dad saving him from the current. "Whoa," his dad said, concerned. "Are you okay?"

Baxter felt himself slip. He was getting lost in his

thoughts. But he couldn't let that happen. If he did, they'd lose for sure.

His muscles tensed and started to burn as he kicked into gear. He reached the end of the pool, flipped, and pushed off in the opposite direction.

A hotel swimming pool. His mom reading while his dad flipped him high into the air. Baxter crashing back into the water with a mighty splash.

Another memory. Another distraction.

But was it?

These were the reasons he loved to swim. It was in these places, with his family, that he chose to be a swimmer. And even though his family was fractured, it didn't mean the memories were something to push aside.

Baxter let the memories flood his mind as he completed the first lap and started the last. He let them fuel him. He used them to motivate him to do his best. The California vacation. His dad splashing him in the pool.

Then other memories filled his mind too. His first day of lessons. His time on the junior varsity team. The day Coach Li called him into his office to tell him he would be swimming varsity.

Each memory, like the breath between strokes, gave him strength. It made him faster. Baxter swam harder. He reached the fourth and final turn and headed for the finish.

Baxter caught a quick glance of the swimmer beside him and knew he'd pulled ahead. But he still couldn't tell how he compared to the rest of the pack. All he could do was keep his rhythm, keep his pace, keep his intensity high.

He closed in on the pool's edge.

Put his hand out.

Kicked furiously.

Five yards.

Come on!

Three.

Two.

One.

His fingers touched the lip of the pool. Baxter quickly flipped his head up and looked at his teammates to see how he'd done. Clark and Luke were hugging each other. Arnold held both fists to the sky.

"How'd we do?" Baxter asked breathlessly. He peeled off his goggles and looked at the rest of the swimmers. Only one other team was celebrating. More swimmers were just reaching the pool's edge, including the team in lane two.

"You did it, Tadpole!" Clark reached down and hauled him out of the water. Luke and Arnold joined them in a team embrace. "Second place!" Clark added.

"We're going to state?" Baxter asked, still struggling to catch his breath.

"We're going to state!" the other three answered as one.

* * *

The excitement of the second-place finish lasted through the meet. When Baxter and the rest of the Edgeview team exited the locker room, a crowd of family and friends were waiting for them.

"Congratulations, my boy!" Tayvon's grandma shouted as she shuffled over and pulled him into an embrace.

Baxter's mom was standing in the crowd, a wide smile on her face. "Great race," she said.

"Thanks, Mom," Baxter said.

He spotted his dad hovering around the edge of the crowd, near one of the aquatic center's trophy cases. His mom must have noticed too.

"It's okay," she said. "Wave him over."

Baxter called out, "Yo, Dad!" His dad saw him, smiled, then wove through the crowd toward them.

"That was pretty spectacular, kiddo," his dad said. "I was so proud."

Baxter smiled. It'd been months since the three of them had been together. He'd forgotten how it felt.

It was like the rest of the crowd had disappeared. The pain was still there, hiding in his chest like a stone. But for a moment, it was the way it used to be. And maybe, with time and care, these moments might be more frequent.

This moment was another in the catalog of memories Baxter could use to fuel himself. The state meet was still a month away. There was a lot of time to prepare, and Baxter couldn't wait to get back into the pool to start.

ABOUT the AUTHOR

Brandon Terrell is the author of numerous children's books, working on such series as Tony Hawk's 900 Revolution and Tony Hawk: Live2Skate, Spine Shivers, Michael Dahl Presents: Phobia, *Sports Illustrated Kids*: Time Machine Magazine, Jim Nasium, and Snoops, Inc. He has also written numerous Jake Maddox books and graphic novels. When not hunched over his laptop, Brandon enjoys watching movies and television, reading, watching and playing baseball, and spending time with his wife and two children at his home in Minnesota.

GLOSSARY

alternate (AWL-tur-nit)—a person who substitutes for another

contagious (kuhn-TAY-juhss)—so irresistible as to be picked up by one person from another

distraction (diss-TRAK-shun)—something that makes it hard to focus or pay attention

momentum (moh-MEN-tuhm)—the force or speed an object or person has when moving

preliminary (pri-LIM-uh-ner-ee)—preparing the way for something important that comes later

propelled (pruh-PELLD)—drove or pushed something forward

separation (SEP-uh-ray-shun)—formal separating of a married couple by agreement but without getting a divorce

spectacular (spek-TAK-yuh-lur)—remarkable or amazing

stagnant (STAG-nuhnt)—foul or polluted as a result of not moving

virtual (VUR-choo-uhl)—near

DISCUSSION QUESTIONS

1. Baxter's family is going through a difficult and uncertain time. How is this situation affecting Baxter's position on the swim team?

2. Baxter is the youngest swimmer on the team. How is this difference shown in the story? Find examples in the text.

3. Through much of the story, Baxter is negatively impacted by his memories. Why is this? And why does he decide to use those memories as motivation in the end?

WRITING PROMPTS

1. Baxter's trip to the ocean affected the way he looked at water and made him want to be a swimmer. Write about an experience when you discovered a sport or activity that you love.

2. Imagine you're a reporter for the school's website and write an article about the outcome of the section finals meet.

3. In the end, Baxter and the Edgeview 400 freestyle relay team make it to the state tournament. Write a scene from the tournament where the team competes. Do they win?

MORE ABOUT SWIMMING

Swimming has been a part of the Summer Olympics since 1896, but it wasn't until the 1912 Olympics in Stockholm, Sweden, that women started to participate in the sport at that level.

The history of swimming stretches back a long time! Egyptian drawings dated from 2500 BC show people swimming. Japan held the first recorded swimming race in the year 36 BC. And England turned swimming into a competitive sport in the 1800s.

American swimmer Michael Phelps holds the record for the most Olympic medals in men's swimming, with a staggering total of 28. Of those, 23 are gold medals. The top women's swimmer is American Jenny Thompson with 12 medals total, 8 of which are gold.

The slowest Olympic swim stroke is the breaststroke. The fastest is the freestyle.

At the Olympics, swimmers use a 50-meter pool, known as a long course pool. The National Collegiate Athletic Association and high school swimming programs use short course pools, which measure 25 yards or 25 meters long.

Olympic-level swimmers train from four to five hours per day, five to seven days a week. Training typically consists of strength and flexibility exercises and swimming six to twelve miles per day.

SWIMMING ACTION,
PICK UP . . .

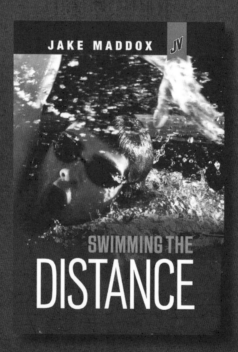